Dear Parent:

Your child's love of reading starts here!

Every child learns to read in a different way and at his or her own speed. Some go back and forth between reading levels and read favorite books again and again. Others read through each level in order. You can help your young reader improve and become more confident by encouraging his or her own interests and abilities. From books your child reads with you to the first books he or she reads alone, there are I Can Read Books for every stage of reading:

SHARED READING
Basic language, word repetition, and whimsical illustrations, ideal for sharing with your emergent reader

BEGINNING READING
Short sentences, familiar words, and simple concepts for children eager to read on their own

READING WITH HELP
Engaging stories, longer sentences, and language play for developing readers

READING ALONE
Complex plots, challenging vocabulary, and high-interest topics for the independent reader

I Can Read Books have introduced children to the joy of reading since 1957. Featuring award-winning authors and illustrators and a fabulous cast of beloved characters, I Can Read Books set the standard for beginning readers.

A lifetime of discovery begins with the magical words "I Can Read!"

*Visit www.icanread.com for information
on enriching your child's reading experience.*

I Can Read® and I Can Read Book® are trademarks of HarperCollins Publishers.
Harold and the Purple Crayon: A New Adventure
TM & © 2022 Columbia Pictures Industries, Inc. All Rights Reserved. Printed in the United States of America.
No part of this book may be used or reproduced in any manner whatsoever without written permission except
in the case of brief quotations embodied in critical articles and reviews. For information address
HarperCollins Children's Books, a division of HarperCollins Publishers, 195 Broadway, New York, NY 10007.
www.icanread.com

Library of Congress Control Number: 2022940803
ISBN 978-0-06-328334-3

22 23 24 25 26   LB   10 9 8 7 6 5 4 3 2 1   ❖   First Edition

HAROLD
and the
PURPLE
CRAYON

A New Adventure

Adapted by Alexandra West
Illustrated by Walter Carzon

HARPER
An Imprint of HarperCollinsPublishers

Once there was a boy named Harold.

He went on lots of adventures.

Harold always brought

his purple crayon along.

Harold's crayon was special.

Whatever Harold drew came to life!

He drew a moon and then a path.

"Follow me!" Harold said.

Harold drew an apple tree.
But everyone knows apple trees
needed a big scary dragon.
So Harold drew that too.

The dragon breathed fire!

"Ahhhh!" Harold yelled.

He was not expecting that.

Harold fell back and

landed in the ocean.

Harold hit a small island!

"Moose!" Harold shouted.

"Porcupine!" Harold yelled.

Harold was excited to see his friends.

"Hi, Harold," Moose said.

"We were just saying

how hungry we were."

Harold raised is purple crayon.

"Say no more," Harold said.

"Pie!" Moose said, excited.

"You remembered my favorite food!"

"Of course I remembered," Harold said.

"You eat it every day."

Harold drew several more pies.

He drew pie after pie until

his friends were full and happy.

Next, Harold began to draw a city.

Building after building,

Harold's city grew bigger and bigger.

The three friends began to explore.

Soon they got lost in the big city.

"Where are we?" Porcupine said.

"Let's ask someone," Harold replied.

Harold drew a policeman

and named him Jeff.

"Can you help us get home?"

Harold asked.

Jeff smiled and pointed to the sky.

The friends looked up.

Jeff was pointing to the moon.

"My bedroom window!" Harold said.

"It's right around the moon!"

17

Harold drew a window around
the moon.

Just like that, they were back
in Harold's bedroom.

What an adventure they'd had!

His friends quickly fell asleep.

Harold climbed into bed.

Harold was fast asleep

before his head hit the pillow.

As Harold's world got bigger,

so did he!

Harold was growing up.

That meant his adventures

became a little more daring.

Harold drew a surfboard

that could fit everyone.

A surfboard needed a giant wave,

so Harold drew that too.

"Surf's up!" Porcupine shouted.

Harold grew more and more.

He was almost an adult.

But Moose and Porcupine

stayed the same.

"I think it's time I learn
to drive," said Harold.

Harold drew a large motorcycle.

"Check out my new ride!"
Harold said.

As Harold grew older,

he also grew more curious.

"I made you guys, right?"

Harold asked Moose and Porcupine.

The two friends nodded.

"But who made me?" Harold asked.

"I did," said a voice.

"Who are you?" Harold said,

looking up into the white sky.

"I'm the narrator," the voice replied.

"I live in the real world."

"Can I go to the real world?"
Harold said.

"Someday," the voice said.

26

Moose and Porcupine were confused.

They had never heard

of the real world before.

But Harold was excited.

It sounded like a new adventure.

Harold liked talking to the narrator.

It was like having a new friend.

But one night, Harold woke up

and something was different.

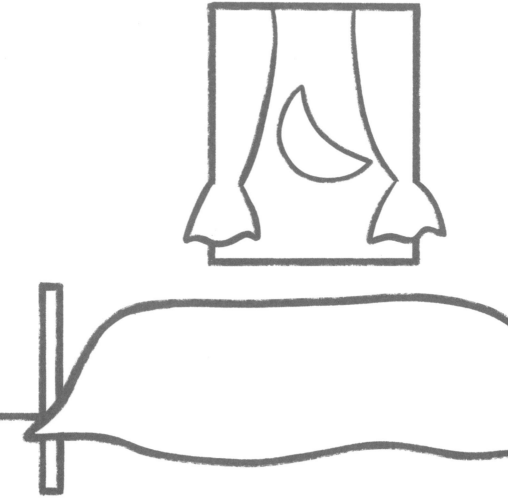

"Hello?" Harold called out.

"Narrator, are you there?"

But there was no answer.

Harold needed to find the narrator.

He decided to go to the real world.

"How do we get there?" Moose asked.

Harold looked at his purple crayon.

"This purple crayon is the key,"
Harold said.

Harold did what he does best.

He began to draw.

Harold drew a purple door

to the real world.

Harold was ready

for his next great adventure.